The Old Dog and the Coyote

By Adán Zepeda
Illustrations by Nancy Glon

Library of Congress Card Number: 2004097174

ISBN: 9651440-3-8

Printed in the United States of America

2000 Evangel Way
Nappanee, IN 46550-0189

Table of Contents

Illustrations

3

THE OLD DOG AND THE COYOTE

Chapter One

It all started early one morning as the family's pet dog, Tiger, lay sleeping on the steps of the Terrell's country home. His master, Don Terrell, who was leaving for work, walked out of the house and down the wooden steps of the front porch where he tripped over the sleeping dog. Falling down the steps and onto the brick sidewalk, he broke his arm, scattering the papers from his briefcase all across the wet grass. "You stupid dog!" he cried out in pain and anger. "Rosa, Rosa! Quick! Come here!" he yelled. His wife heard his cries and hurried out to help him. Because Don Terrell was a big man, it was difficult for his wife to help him get up, and that didn't make her husband any less angry either. She finally managed to get him into the house and then to the doctor.

Tiger took off running. He crawled under the floor of the back porch, whimpering in pain. When he tripped, the master had stepped on the dog's belly and had surely broken one of his ribs. Tiger finally stopped whimpering and lay silent in the dark shadow and safety under the porch knowing he was in big trouble because he had never heard his master sound so angry. Until Mr. Terrell's temper had cooled down, Tiger knew he should stay out of sight.

There was another problem besides being the cause of his master's accident: Tiger's age. Mr. Terrell had often complained during the last couple of years that the old dog was "in the way" and "wasn't doing his job". As a young dog, Tiger had been a warrior, the protector of the house and property and a guardian of the Terrell children. No other animals or neighboring dogs would dare to trespass on his territory. Anyone who came to visit the family respected Tiger because he was so aggressive in the defense of his master's property. It seemed to the old dog that Don Terrell had forgotten all about that. And today's accident had made things even worse.

Because the master's arm was so badly broken and he had suffered so many bruises, he was forced to stay home for several weeks. He couldn't work, which meant no paycheck. He couldn't even keep up with the chores and repairs around the house and yard. During that time, his attitude toward Tiger became even worse.

As for Tiger, he continued to hide under the porch every day, trying to sleep and letting his bruises heal. He didn't come out to bark at visitors or even the mailman's car. The rabbits ran everywhere but Tiger paid no attention. Even hearing the coyote's howl off in the woods didn't tempt him to come out from his place of safety. Only Rosa, the master's wife, had any sympathy for him. She managed to slip him some food whenever her husband was taking a nap or watching television.

Tiger was supposed to be guarding the chickens, too. For many years, the Terrell's children had been involved with 4-H and had raised prize chickens. Roosters and hens came out of the coop every morning to peck at the seeds and bugs around the yard. When coyotes tried to sneak in to steal a chicken or two, Tiger had always been on the job protecting the flock from those thieves—until now. He neither growled nor lifted his head when the coyotes appeared at the edge of the woods, and they became increasingly bolder.

The good days were all in the past. The children were grown with families of their own. No one called, "Here, Tiger. Here, Tiger. Come on, Fluffy Bones." No one patted him on the head and said, "Good dog," anymore, and no one played for hours with him throwing a ball or a stick for him to fetch. He was just an old dog, too old to be any good for anything. The pleasant moments of happier days lingered only in Tiger's memory. Things were different now and couldn't get any worse. That's what the old dog thought. But he was wrong.

Chapter Two

It was a few weeks after the accident and very early in the morning—too early for the sun to be up. There was just enough light so that the world appeared to be gray and the shadows were still dark. The Terrells were sleeping and Tiger lay curled up in the dust under the porch.

Suddenly, there was a loud commotion coming from the chicken coop. The squawking of the hens and roosters and the loud flapping of their wings awakened Tiger and his master at the same time.

Rosa and Don jumped out of bed and hurried to see what was causing the disturbance. Still wearing their pajamas, they ran to the door calling," Tiger, Tiger! Go! Go get it, Tiger! Go get the intruder!" But Tiger didn't respond. He remained in his place of safety, still remembering his master's anger. He didn't want to go see what was making so much noise so he didn't see the clever coyote that slipped through the shadows, then took the fattest chicken in the hen house. The chickens were always too noisy. They sometimes got excited when a little wind blew the leaves—they'd quiet down soon. So, the old dog went back to sleep.

After the sun came up and it was light enough to see inside the coop, the Terrells dressed and went out to check the flock. Two dead chickens were found inside the coop and they discovered that the coyote had taken Rosa's best hen. Don was furious. He blamed Tiger for the loss of the chickens and yelled the old dog's name repeatedly and walked around with his rifle in his good hand and the barrel resting on the cast on his broken arm. "That darn dog," he said. "He'd better not show up right now because I'll shoot him if he does." Tiger could hear the angry words and stayed hidden, crawling even further under the back porch, in the corner near the kitchen floor. He was afraid of what his master was going to do to him now.

"I don't know where that stupid dog is, but if he is under the porch, I hope he doesn't die under there because I would have to crawl under and drag him out," Don said.

Rosa tried to calm her husband by saying, "Well, he is an old dog, you know. Maybe we should start looking for a younger dog. Perhaps you should call the humane society to come and pick up Tiger before he does die under the porch."

"That's for sure. If I don't shoot him myself, we definitely need to get rid of him," her husband responded. Then, Mr. Terrell went straight to the telephone and made a call—not to the humane society, but to some raccoon hunters he knew who would take care of Tiger once and for all and he would be glad to pay them to do it.

The wooden floor over the old dog's head made it possible for Tiger to hear every word being said, and he trembled in fear at the anger in the master's voice. He knew that his life could be over very soon if he didn't do something to save himself. Tiger trusted Mrs. Terrell not to hurt him, but as long as the master had said to get rid of him, she had to agree. Don Terrell made the decisions in their home and there were no ifs, ands or buts once he made up his mind.

Tiger had to decide what to do next. Should he run away into the woods and never come back? Then he remembered his enemies, the sly, clever coyotes. He knew they could tear him apart in the same way he had done to a careless young coyote that had dared to come into his territory long ago. Running into the nearby town wasn't a good idea, either, because of Tiger's fearsome reputation, although he had simply done his job. He had only wanted to protect his own territory when he chased other dogs away. To get revenge, surrounding dogs would be ready to fight him. It was an unhappy conclusion, but he realized that he was at the end of the rope—that he was an old dog—but he didn't want to die yet.

On the day the master was able to return to work, he still sounded angry as he told Rosa, "Don't forget about that telephone call I made to the raccoon hunters. They are coming today." Then he climbed into his truck and drove off.

Chapter Three

Shortly after that, Rosa came out of the house to feed the chickens. She also brought some food for Tiger. "Come here, Tiger," she called with a soft voice. "Come on, boy, I have your breakfast." But Tiger was reluctant to come out from under the porch. Maybe it was the decision to get rid of him that made her voice sound guilty. "Come on, Tiger. I have your breakfast. It's sausage, toast and milk— something special just for you." But Tiger was suspicious. Was this the master's breakfast that he hadn't eaten because he was still angry? Or had she prepared this as Tiger's last meal? Again she called his name, "Come on out here, Tiger; come on, old boy. Here's a drink of water for you, too."

Slowly, Tiger came out from under the porch. He knew Don was gone, but he was still afraid. His eyes were sad and his tail was between his legs as he approached Rosa. The broken ribs still hurt, but he also knew that they no longer wanted him around. And that hurt him, too. His aged head was low and his pain was so apparent, that Rosa's eyes filled with tears as she patted his head and placed his food on the ground in front of him. Softly she said, "Thanks, Tiger, for being such a good dog and part of our family all these years." Tiger only looked at her with his unhappy eyes, sad in his own way at how things had turned out. The old dog slowly ate the food, lapped a little of the water, then turned toward the back porch where he planned to crawl underneath to hide and sleep again.

Before he could get there, however, an old truck pulled into the driveway. He had never seen this truck before, but he didn't bother to bark at it. What was the use? If they were going to take him away, he'd just crawl under the porch, and go far back in the corner where he had hidden from the master. Maybe they wouldn't be able to reach him and pull him out—no matter how they tried.

He listened and heard a man's voice asking for directions. It was a false alarm. They weren't here for Tiger after all. Feeling a little better, he took a good nap and didn't awaken until about noon.

The sun was warm and, since Don was still at work, Tiger felt relaxed enough to come out from his hiding place. Walking around the yard on his old, stiff legs, sniffing here and there, his tail wagging a little, the dog marked his territory again as he had done so many times over the years. He heard Rosa call and watched her as she crossed the yard toward him. She held a hamburger in one hand, but her other hand was hidden behind her back. The meat smelled good, and Tiger accepted it, eating quickly. He looked up at Rosa, trusting her, and she patted him on his head.

He was enjoying the silky touch of her hand when suddenly the leash was snapped onto his collar and she had captured him. He tried to run, but it was too late. As Rosa pulled on him, he refused to walk, so she dragged him across the yard where she tied him to a tree near the driveway. Then she went into the house. His heart broken, Tiger cried, but no one listened. He could still taste the hamburger—that meat that had deceived him. He had trusted Rosa once too often.

Later, Rosa came out of the house with the car keys in her hand. She didn't look at Tiger as she got into the car and drove down the driveway and out onto the road. He knew she didn't want to be there when the men came to get him. Tiger whimpered and cried as he watched her car disappear.

Chapter Four

The poor old dog could never remember a time when he had been so unhappy. He lay down with his head on his paws waiting for those he knew would soon come to take him away.

It was early afternoon, when another pick-up truck pulled into the yard. The old dog raised his head to watch and saw a big cage in the back. Two ugly looking men got

"...the other one grabbed his neck and tail."

21

out of the truck. Both of the men were dirty with long, shaggy hair and neither one had shaved his beard for several days. They had also been drinking. Tiger could smell them from where he was tied, and he growled as they approached. However, he had no choice in what was going to happen and gave them no resistance at all. One of the men untied the leash from the tree, holding it short, while the other one grabbed Tiger's neck and tail. They didn't bother to use the long pole with the wire loop.

"He's sure a skinny old mutt, ain't he, Bob?" said one. And sure enough, the forty-five pound, old, skinny dog was easy to pick up. Carrying him to the truck, they simply threw him into the cage with his leash still attached to his collar as they slammed the wire door shut. The men didn't lock it because Tiger was too old to give them any trouble.

The man called Bob said, "I hate picking up other people's dogs. I don't know why we have to keep doing it."

"Well, it's a pretty easy fifty bucks. All we have to do is take 'em to the woods, shoot 'em and dump the carcass in the weeds. The coyotes do the rest," responded the second man.

"Yeah, I guess you're right. Well, let's get out of here."

They drove away, spinning the wheels of the truck and kicking up gravel in the road as they left.

The men continued drinking, and their driving became increasingly reckless. Tiger could see their rifles in a rack in the cab of the truck that they used to shoot raccoons and rabbits—and probably old dogs, too. However, Tiger was left in the cage when they stopped to check their traps. He had no water to drink and the dusty roads and the hot afternoon sun made him very thirsty. Each time he heard gunshots in the woods, he wondered when those rifles would be used on him.

Time passed and the driving became worse, and Tiger bounced around in the cage in the back of the truck, falling and sliding against the wires that hurt his body every time he hit the sides. All afternoon and into the early evening, the men drove around from woods to woods checking traps and shooting at rabbits, though they never brought one back with them. They had continued to drink, and Tiger was very tired, dizzy and bruised from their dangerous driving.

Tiger had no idea how far from home they had driven, but it was getting dark and he believed they had probably traveled a very long way—maybe even a hundred miles. The voices of the two men were getting louder. They had begun to argue about money. Tiger didn't understand the exact problem but he heard Mr. Terrell's name mentioned several times.

The truck had been weaving from side to side on the gravel road, and suddenly they skidded and rolled over.

The pickup landed in a ditch upside down with the wheels in the air. The cage was thrown out of the back with Tiger still inside. The cage door popped open as it landed and Tiger suddenly had his chance for freedom again.

Chapter Five

Having no idea where he was, Tiger ran toward the trees in front of him. He looked over his shoulder and realized that the two men didn't come after him because they had their own set of problems now. Maybe these woods would be a good place to hide or die peacefully even if he was far away from the home he loved so much.

Running as fast as his old bruised bones could carry him, he jumped over a fallen tree and didn't notice his leash catching in a split in the wood until it jerked him to a stop, causing him to fall to the ground. Tiger struggled to stand up, legs spread, tongue hanging out, panting for breath. He pulled on the leash to get away, but the more he struggled, the tighter it was caught. Pulling on it only choked him. By then, most of his energy was gone and he felt exhausted. There had been no naps in the wire cage and running from the men had taken the last of his strength.

It was getting darker and cooler, too since the sun had already gone down. The shadows of the trees and little disturbances in the woods—crickets, owls and crawly things—were beginning to make Tiger a little nervous. His hearing was still sharp and he listened to all the strange sounds, especially the howling of the coyote off in the distance. Walking around in the dead leaves by the tree, he made a little bed for himself, but the unusual noises kept him from sleeping well in this strange place.

Then he heard a different sound and Tiger lifted his head, cocking his ears. There was something coming through the woods. It was being very quiet and coming slowly, but he could hear it. Whatever was coming, was approaching through the dry leaves, but what? As the sound came closer, he didn't know if he should growl or bark. If he barked, the coyotes might hear him. He sniffed the air trying to figure out what the intruder was. But neither his sense of smell nor his hearing helped him. As he listened, the noise stopped for a while. Then, again it began moving.

Tiger breathed nervously and tried to see in the darkness. His ears and eyes were straining when he was finally able to recognize a familiar shape. An old box turtle was rustling through the leaves paying no attention to the dog whose leash was caught in the fallen tree. The old dog breathed a sigh of relief. Finally, because he was old and weak from having no food or water, Tiger slept.

Because he was so tired, it was afternoon before he awakened again. He realized it must be the next day. Again, he tried to break loose, but without success. Every time he struggled, he became exhausted and had to stop to rest. Also, with the leash pulled so tight around his neck he couldn't reach it to chew it through.

One by one the hours slipped by and Tiger fell asleep again until his thirst awakened him. He found a piece of green stick by the fallen tree and chewed on it a little to help him feel less thirsty. More time passed. That night, Tiger believed he was truly going to die. Two days with neither food nor water was a long time for such an old dog. He heard the coyotes howl again, closer this time and he was afraid they were going to find him. There was nothing he could do, but wait. He might sleep again, and maybe not wake up this time.

Three days had passed. Tiger had lost all hope of escaping although he was glad he was still alive. He chewed on another stick for a little while which did seem to help his thirst somewhat. There was nothing left but to lie down and wait for the unknown future.

Chapter Six

The sun was high in the sky when an unusual noise awakened him, and he saw that he was surrounded by those he feared most, a pack of coyotes. "Please, don't kill me!" he whimpered.

The leader of the pack stepped forward growling and snarled, "What do you think you're doing here in our territory?" Tiger heard the anger and fierce authority in the voice of the coyote.

32

"I'm sorry to have invaded your territory," Tiger said, "but I am supposed to be dead."

The coyote did not understand why Tiger said that and approached the dog, ready to fight. However, as the leader walked around Tiger, he saw the leash that was caught and tangled. He realized that the dog had no way to get free or defend himself. The coyote knew that a leash on his own neck would have kept him from being free. Only a human would tie a leash on a dog that was running in the woods. He also could see that Tiger was old and very skinny. Tying him up seemed to be a cruel thing for a human to do. The coyote decided to find out more about this old dog.

Tiger put his head down on his paws waiting for the coyotes to attack him. "Who are you and who brought you here?" demanded the leader.

"It is a long story," answered Tiger, sitting up. "My name is Tiger and some men were going to shoot me but they had an accident with their truck and I managed to escape."

"Why were they going to kill you?"

"I am too old to be any good as a protector of my family's home and property, so my master decided to have me killed," explained Tiger.

The coyote leader commanded the rest of the pack to leave while he stayed to talk to the old dog. Tiger told the story about his master tripping over him, and how angry he had been at the faithful, family pet. "A few days after that, an intruder came during the early morning, killed two chickens and stole the fattest hen from the coop, and I didn't stop the thief. That's when they said I was no good and arranged to have me killed," Tiger told the coyote.

The clever coyote knew the old dog was telling the truth because he had been the intruder in the chicken coop that night—although he never admitted the true story to Tiger.

"Look here, Old Dog, I think I can help you."

Tiger didn't believe the coyote very much; he thought the coyote wanted to see him dead with the leash still around his neck, but he decided to listen. At least the coyote had not attacked him or allowed the rest of the pack to hurt him either. It gave the dog a little hope, so he responded, "Well, if you are willing to help me, maybe I'll be able to do something to help you, too, although I don't know how I'll repay you."

"I'll be back in the morning," said Coyote, and he left without explaining his intentions. He had a plan in his mind that would certainly help him as well as the dog. For that night, however, Tiger was left alone again and still a prisoner in the woods without food or water.

Chapter Seven

The old dog was surprised when the coyote returned the
next day, because he was already prepared to die of thirst.
Tiger listened to the coyote that asked him, "Are you sure
you don't know where you are?"

"How could I know? Those men had me on their truck
all afternoon, driving around from one woods to another.
They drove for miles and miles, and so recklessly that I was
too dizzy to know where I was."

" Well, let me tell you something, Old Dog, you are not too far away from your home. It's just on the other side of this woods."

"Really?" Tiger said. He became very excited at this piece of news. But added, "Of course that doesn't do me much good because they don't want me there anyway. I wish I could do something that would change their minds again," he said sadly, hanging his head.

"Do you think you could come up with a plan?" asked Coyote with a sly look in his eyes.

"What do you mean, 'a plan'?" asked Tiger. He was too thirsty to be thinking about different strategies.

"Well," said Coyote looking at Tiger, "we all need to have a plan if we want to survive. I might have one that would work, but you would have to be willing to cooperate with me to make it work."

All Tiger could think about was the leash that was still caught in the fallen tree and holding him captive. He simply wanted to be free. If the coyote wanted to help him get loose, that was wonderful, but the dog had no way of knowing what he was planning in addition.

The smart coyote did indeed want to help Tiger, but more than that he was thinking of helping himself as well. "I'm going to get something to eat," said Coyote walking away once more, "but I'll be back."

"What about me?" yelped Tiger. "I'm hungry and thirsty, too." He was very disappointed to see the coyote leave again and he still didn't have his freedom. But the smart coyote knew what he was doing. He didn't want to free Tiger until he knew for sure that the old dog would help him.

As Coyote vanished into the woods for the second time, Tiger felt even lonelier. Discouraged, he could stand no longer. The leash pulled tight around his neck, but he lay down with his head on his paws. He slept again, but began to dream about the times when he was a little puppy playing with the Terrell children, whimpering as he slept.

He dreamed about Mr. Terrell bringing him home when he was only six weeks old. He remembered having to leave his brothers and sisters who were left with his mother.

The little puppy was a mixed breed, so no one could tell which particular kind he really was. However, because he had some funny looking stripes on his tummy, the family decided to name him Tiger.

Chapter Eight

The children had been crazy about their new family member. No matter what they ate, Tiger was allowed to have some, too. Whatever he begged for, they gave him—cookies, potato chips, hot dogs, plenty of milk and anything else he wanted. Mrs. Terrell would sometimes put him in the bathtub with the children and he would swim and splash in the water. The children thought he was very funny when he was wet.

One time, he was sleeping in the top bunk and fell out all the way to the floor. He cried and cried, so the little girl, Marta, put him in bed with her on the bottom bunk. After that, he always slept with her. He remembered how good she smelled and she was always so gentle, too.

When the children went to school, Tiger would meet them on their way home. They were always happy to see him and gave him little bites of crunchy candy for a treat.

He dreamed that he grew bigger and had to sleep outside. His job was to protect the interests of the family and in his dream, he barked to warn the master when coyotes came near or when he heard them howl.

He saw the children as they grew older when they raised chickens for 4-H at the fair. Tiger had loved taking care of those crazy hens and roosters. He learned how to round them up to make them go inside the chicken coop at night, but it was fun to make them fly around, flapping their wings and making a lot of noise, too. Taking care of his responsibilities had made him an important member of the family.

He dreamed about the family cookouts, when he was allowed to have his own juicy steak and maybe some leftovers, too. He always had plenty of water to drink in his own bowl so he never had to go thirsty either.

Dreaming about the steaks and the water made Tiger wake up. He had never been so hungry and thirsty, and he remembered that he was still trapped in the woods with the leash still caught tight. Looking through the trees, he saw the coyote coming again. Probably he was coming to kill him at last, but Tiger didn't care any more. He had given up.

This time, however, Tiger was wrong. The coyote had brought something to eat. It was half a rabbit and it was all for Tiger. He didn't ask questions, he just attacked that meat immediately, devouring it but being careful to avoid getting the fur in his mouth. "That was good," he said when he'd finished. "I've never tasted rabbit before. Thank you, Coyote. I feel much better."

"Have you ever tasted chicken?" asked Coyote.

"No," answered Tiger, "but I'm not sure I'd like them. Too many feathers."

"Oh, you'd like them if you ever ate one. You're very hungry so the rabbit tasted good. But chickens are very tasty, too," said Coyote, licking his mouth with his long tongue. "I know that from my own experience."

Now that Tiger had eaten his meal, he had a little more energy, and was curious to hear about the plan the coyote had mentioned. How the coyote could help Tiger was something he was anxious to learn—he also wanted to know how soon he would be free.

The coyote seemed very friendly now. "Before I tell you what I have in mind, let me set you free." He quickly bit the leather leash in two and the old dog was no longer a prisoner.

"This feels wonderful to be free again," Tiger said with sincere gratitude, walking around, stretching his legs and wagging his tail.

"Remember," said the coyote, "since I helped you, you must help me. First we will go to the creek where you can get a drink, then we will talk."

"Of course," said the old dog."You just tell me what to do and I'll do it." Then, they ran to get some water and Tiger drank for a long time. Water had never tasted so cool and delicious. He was feeling very grateful toward this new friend, and it no longer mattered that it was a coyote.

"Now, follow me through the woods and I will show you the way to your home."

So, the coyote led the way and Tiger followed him.
Sure enough, Coyote knew exactly where Tiger had lived.
At the edge of the woods, they stopped and looked out
across the open grass toward the chicken coop. Tiger could
see the old back porch and the tree in front where Rosa had
tied him. They didn't walk out into the open, but stayed
hidden behind the bushes and weeds. Coyote cautioned
Tiger to stay behind him. They both knew the danger of
being shot if they were seen.

"Do you see those chickens?" asked Coyote.

"Yes, but they don't belong to me," answered Tiger,
"they belong to my master."

"Well, you will be able to have one if you listen to my
plan."

"But I don't want to get shot," said Tiger. "Have you
ever been close to that place before? They have a rifle and
often shoot at coyotes."

"Okay, go get one."

"I've seen the chickens many times," answered the clever coyote, turning back toward the woods. "Come on, those chickens are too tempting for me," he said looking back over his shoulder at the flock of hens and roosters scratching in the dirt.

Tiger looked back, too, but not because he wanted the chickens; he wanted to go home. Then Coyote said, "How would you like to try some chicken for lunch?" Tiger didn't much like the idea, but didn't want to argue with the coyote. He was still a little afraid of his new friend.

"Okay, go get one," he said, "I think I could eat a little more." Tiger didn't have to tell Coyote twice. Leaving the dog in the woods, Coyote took off. No one seemed to be at the Terrell's house, and while Tiger watched, the coyote circled around the coop and in less than five minutes, he was back with a nice fresh chicken. It was the coyote's favorite meal, but he willingly shared it with Tiger on the edge of the woods behind the bushes. The dog had liked the rabbit, but the chicken tasted good, too.

The old dog was used to taking a nap after a meal, and now he was really sleepy. After the two of them had walked back into the woods, Tiger suggested that they take a little nap, but Coyote said, "No. No one is going to catch me sleeping. Humans might come looking for me with a gun and, if I'm sleeping, they'll catch me easily. No. Not me. Come on, I want to tell you my plan."

Chapter Nine

Tiger knew Coyote was smart and he knew he should listen to his teacher.

"Tonight," Coyote instructed him, "you will go to your house and hide in the place you think is the best. Wait until it's very late and the house is dark and quiet. Make sure no one sees you or where you're hiding."

He continued, "Don't come out until tomorrow when you see me and hear me chasing the chickens all around the yard and making a lot of noise. Then, you can run out and start chasing me around the chicken coop. I'll let you catch me and we will fight each other—not a real fight, just a friendly fight. But it needs to look real."

"What if Mrs. Terrell comes out with her gun? What happens then?" asked Tiger.

"That's a chance we'll have to take. I don't think she will shoot you anyway," said the coyote.

"Boy, this is risky business," Tiger said seriously.

"Yes, it is, but without risks, you never get anything worthwhile," said the coyote wisely. "Just remember, it will be a fake fight—not real. Otherwise, you'll be sorry we ever met," he warned. He looked at Tiger right in the eyes when he said this. Then he said, "When your mistress shows up, I'll run into the woods, but you must keep chasing me so it looks as if you are really getting rid of me. Later, when it gets dark, I'll come back and you can tell me how they treat you. And that is when you can pretend to chase me, but you will always allow me to be able to catch one or two chickens."

"Wow, that sounds like it might work. But what makes you so smart?" asked Tiger. "How do you know so much?"

"I think we have learned so much because we have to survive by ourselves," answered Coyote. "You are domestic and we are born in the wild. You have someone to care for you, feed you and even take you to a veterinarian when you are sick. We have no one to help us. No one will feed us. So, we have to take care of ourselves. Humans are our enemies and want to kill us because we eat their chickens, ducks and sometimes even a goat or two. They don't realize we only take their animals because we have to survive.

"At night, when the men come to hunt us with flashlights, we don't look at the light; we stay far away and only allow one eye to show. In that way, the light doesn't blind us as it blinds other animals because they show both eyes at the same time. We know better."

"That is a magnificent idea," exclaimed the dog.

"Some people try to trick us in different ways. Sometimes they hide traps in a hole in the ground and cover them with leaves and dirt. Then, they hang a piece of meat from a tree branch to tempt us. Fortunately, we can smell those humans who have been there and we pull the trap out of the dirt. Then we can jump up to grab the hanging meat. Young coyotes sometimes are caught, but as we grow older, we know these things. Sometimes, if a piece of meat is lying on the ground, we do not eat it. We can smell the poison the humans put on it and we will not touch it. Only the inexperienced young pups might eat it. They will be the ones who die."

The old dog looked at Coyote and listened carefully as his friend explained the ways of survival. "I don't think I'd ever make it if I had to live in the wild," Tiger said respectfully. "You are very smart and I admire you, my friend. Many times I have chased a rabbit, but I was never able to catch one."

"There are times when we coyotes work together as a team, too. That is usually when we are hungry for a tender goat. It is more difficult to catch larger animals because they are in a herd and guarded by a shepherd who has a rifle and one or two dogs. The first thing we do is try to get close to the goats, but remain hidden behind the bushes, so we can watch the man near the gun. When we are almost ready to attack the goat, one of us boldly walks out into the open where the man can see him. The man picks up his rifle and walks toward him. Then, of course, the coyote disappears into the shadows of the bushes. A little later, that same coyote shows up again but farther away. The rifleman follows him but tells his dogs to stay with the herd. We continue to lead the shepherd farther away always keeping him away from the goats. Finally, when the shepherd is far enough away, the rest of the pack attacks the goat they have selected. Sometimes one of us must fight with the dogs, too. If that happens, another one of us takes the goat far away—then, we all gather to eat our meal."

"It is good to share," Tiger said, but I have a question. "When you kill a goat, do you have to drag it all the way to where you feel safe enough to eat it? It seems as if it would be very heavy to do that." Coyote looked at Tiger when he had finished asking his question. He was very confident and sat up straight staring at the old dog before he answered.

"Oh, no, my friend. We know how to carry a larger goat but not many others have seen our trick. After the goat has been killed, we get a good grip on its throat with our teeth. By jerking our head to one side, we manage to flip the goat on our back to carry it as we run, but we still keep holding on to the throat. Although our head is turned far to the side, we can still see in front of us with one eye as we run. It is not an easy task, but we have learned how to do it successfully. Of course, if it is a small animal, we still carry it in front of us as we run."

Tiger was amazed at the tricks the coyote had learned to play on the humans to obtain food. "You are very intelligent," he said, "to be able to survive so well."

"It is just teamwork," responded Coyote. "In the same way I helped you here in the woods so you didn't die, my friends and family help each other so we can live in the wild without help from the humans."

"You are right," said Tiger, "and I certainly do thank you for all you have done to keep me alive. If you still want me to do something in return, I will certainly try my best to do it. I have no other way to pay you." However, the dog was afraid that the coyote's plan to get the chickens might not work. He kept remembering that his master had a gun and knew very well how to use it.

Chapter Ten

Soon, Coyote said, "I'm hungry; I'm going to find something to eat."

"I am starving," said Tiger, "but I won't be able to catch anything to eat; I'm too old and slow." Part of a rabbit and part of a chicken after almost three days wasn't much to eat.

"Well," said Coyote, "that may be a problem for you, but maybe I can help you again. It would be a good idea if you continue to think about helping me with the chickens. They are the easiest way to have something to eat." Then he left again disappearing into the shadows of the bushes and trees.

As the time passed, and the old dog became hungrier and hungrier, Tiger hoped the turtle might come back. He didn't realize that his old teeth would never be able to penetrate the shell on that slow moving creature. All he could think about was something to eat and the turtle might be something tasty.

Just as quietly as he had disappeared earlier, Coyote reappeared, carrying something in his mouth. He lay it down on the ground in front of Tiger. "What is that?" asked the dog. "It looks like an ugly, hairy rat."

"That's just what it is. Eat it," said Coyote.

Tiger had no choice. It was like medicine—something you have to take for your own good. After he had eaten, Tiger thought to himself, *"My friend was right. Chicken is a hundred times tastier than a rat, and, if I have to choose between the two, I certainly understand why Coyote wanted me to taste chicken first. However, eating something is certainly better than going hungry—even an ugly, hairy rat."*

"Do you still remember our plan about the chickens?" asked Coyote realizing that the old dog didn't like having to eat the rat for a meal.

"Oh, yes," said Tiger with a slightly uncomfortable feeling and remembering the tasty chicken and the different taste of the rat. And he was thinking about returning to the home where he was not welcome. "Do you really think your plan will work?" he asked with hope in his voice.

"To be honest," answered Coyote, "I don't know. But we have to try something and this is certainly the best plan right now."

"You have to remember that I am old, and it's my life in the balance," whined Tiger sadly with a little fear in his voice. "You know how to survive and it is easier for you."

"You can't give up," said Coyote wisely. "You must never give up. You must have faith and trust and a lot of self-confidence. But never give up. Besides," said the coyote, "I am your friend and friends help each other. And, keep in mind, the chickens you help me get will be the way you can pay me back for helping you."

"You're right again, my friend," said Tiger with a little better feeling. "It's better to help you get a few of those chickens than to lose my own life out here in these woods."

"Now, I have another question for you, Coyote," said Tiger. "How do you manage to get the chickens when they are roosting in the trees?"

"Oh, boy," said the coyote rolling his eyes. "Don't you even know how to do that?"

With a proud voice he said, "I very quietly sneak up under the trees where the chickens are roosting. I move slowly, trying not to scare them. When they do see me, I only move my tail back and forth, back and forth, until they are hypnotized. Then, they simply let go of the branch and fall out of the tree and I catch them." Then he added, "When the chickens are in the coop, it's a different matter—especially if there is a dog around. Only this time you will be there to help me."

Tiger was again amazed at the power these coyotes had in surviving. He was fascinated with the secrets Coyote had told him, but also concerned about the plan and how it would really turn out. He thought Coyote might be expecting too much from such an old dog. Although the coyote had truly saved his life, perhaps he was counting on too many chickens in return.

Coyote was watching Tiger who had started scratching his shoulder, and he asked, "You're not thinking of backing out, are you?"

"Oh, no," said Tiger guiltily, "but I sure do wish I could get rid of these fleas. They have gotten worse since I've been here in the woods. Usually my master takes me to the veterinarian's office where they treat my fleas with medicine to get rid of them."

"We have our own way to get rid of those itchy bugs," said his friend. Once more, Tiger was about to learn something important about survival. "We have to find some water that is deep enough to cover our body," began Coyote, "like the creek where we drank the water when you were thirsty. Then we begin to enter the water by backing into it, tail first. The fleas start moving up toward our back and shoulders. Then we back in a little deeper until, finally, only our nose is sticking out of the water. At the end, we put our head completely under the water and by that time, all the fleas are off and drowned in the water."

"I just can't believe how smart you are," exclaimed Tiger with a respectful voice. "How did you learn so much?" he asked.

"One of the most important things we learn when we are only pups, is to listen to the old ones in our pack. They know many things and teach us how to survive while we are very young. They teach us all the things I have told you. There are some in our pack that neither listen nor learn. They are the ones who don't survive. Sometimes they are chased out of the pack to live on their own because they bring the threat of danger to the rest of us."

"My friend, Coyote, that is a beautiful story and very educational for me. I thank you for the experience of listening to you. You are a good teacher," said Tiger. "I have learned a lot from you. My own story is so different.

The Terrells were my only family because I was taken from my mother, brothers and sisters when I was very small. No one of my own kind taught me anything."

Chapter Eleven

Coyote and Tiger had talked for a long time and the sun had already set. However, before the plan could be put into action, it would have to be midnight and almost total darkness. Neither of the two animals wanted to risk being seen. Then coyote left to join his pack for the night saying, "Remember, I'll see you in the morning."

The long hours passed slowly, the moon rose and Tiger grew restless. He could hear the howling of the pack of coyotes and the sound made him especially anxious. Finally, at midnight, Tiger slipped through the woods, across the yard and underneath the back porch to hide and wait for the next step. Everything was just as he remembered it had been under the darkened porch— peaceful and tranquil. Before long, he was asleep.

He didn't know how long he had slept, but he awakened when he heard the sound of Rosa's steps on the wooden floor of the kitchen. Then the familiar smell of coffee, bacon and eggs made him aware that he was hungry again. A few minutes later, the sound of heavier footsteps told him that his master, Don Terrell, was coming to eat. Tiger could easily hear the husband and wife talking as they sat at the table—his ears were his best tools. They talked about the grandchildren who had visited for a while just yesterday. He heard them discussing the day's chores and about the new dog. Tiger put his head on his paws and listened. Having a new dog to take his place made him feel sad. He heard them say that a ninety-five pound, young German shepherd would be delivered in three or four days.

Although it was foggy and the sun hadn't appeared yet, the cock was crowing in the chicken coop assuring the world that it was going to be a beautiful day. By the time Mr. Terrell left for work, the old dog felt a little better. He had felt uncomfortable knowing his master was just over his head. Too, he was wondering what reaction Mrs. Terrell would have when she discovered that Tiger was back home.

A short time later, she came out to feed the chickens, first looking all around the outside of the chicken coop. She checked under it and then looked at the woods to be sure it was safe to let the chickens loose. Then she opened the door to the coop and the chickens came flying out all over the yard. They squawked and flapped their wings, making dust and feathers fly in the morning sun.

Tiger didn't move and held his breath afraid Rosa would look under the porch and find him, which would certainly spoil everything he and the coyote had planned. Now the chickens looked tempting to him, too. His eyes followed Rosa Terrell as she continued to watch her flock. She looked over at the woods again, watching for coyotes.

The sun rose slowly behind the woods where great patches of fog seemed to settle. Rosa finally went into the house, but Tiger was getting jumpy just knowing that the coyote was coming—but not knowing exactly when. He stuck his head out from under the porch to see if he could spot his friend. Some chickens saw Tiger and started clucking and making loud noises. Rosa came running with the rifle in her hand. Fortunately, she didn't see anything and decided it was just a false alarm. Tiger crawled quietly back into the shadows.

The morning passed too slowly for Tiger and he was feeling like a prisoner again. It was about ten o'clock and chickens were scattered all over the yard scratching for bugs and seeds in the dirt. The woods were about two hundred yards away where his friend, Coyote, would be. Tiger waited and watched. Then, suddenly, he heard a commotion. Chickens were running and flying up in the air and in all directions and there was Coyote chasing after a young chicken.

Catching chickens was always a challenge for the coyote, and today was no different—still a dangerous mission. Tiger came out from under the porch, growling like a lion and began chasing the coyote. He forced his old legs to carry him as fast as he could. The chickens didn't know which way to go to hide and continued to flap their wings in confusion, running in every direction. Tiger followed the coyote all around the coop knocking down shovels and scattering the charcoal for the grill. Baskets

went tumbling and tools fell to the ground before he caught

up with his friend.

" *Get him, Tiger, get him!*"

Chapter Twelve

By the time Rosa came running out of the house, the first thing she saw was Tiger fighting with the coyote. The coyote was trying to defend himself from her dog, her Tiger that she thought was dead. She didn't know what to think. Of course, both Tiger and the coyote were trying their best to keep to the plan, pretending to fight fiercely. Rosa's knees were shaking, but she yelled, "Get him, Tiger! Get him!" The dog and coyote wrestled each other rolling over and over looking as if they were having a real fight. They growled and snapped as they fought. Finally,

Rosa remembered to aim the rifle, but as she pointed it toward them anticipating a shot at the coyote, she had trouble getting a clear shot. She wanted desperately to shoot that animal that had been stealing her chickens.

Unfortunately, they were rolling over and over so much and Tiger was on the top so often, that she was afraid to shoot for fear of hitting the old dog.

The fight went on and on, and now Tiger was losing his energy and the coyote was on top more, apparently winning the fight. Rosa moved closer to the tangle of animals. She pointed the gun at the coyote and pulled the trigger. Click. Click. Nothing happened. She tried again. Click. Click. Her anger and frustration grew as she watched the coyote that she believed was hurting her Tiger and no bullets would come from the old gun! She took two steps forward and threw the gun at the coyote, but he turned so quickly that she hit Tiger instead. Tiger yelped so loud with his pain, that the coyote was scared and ran off, but not before he snatched a chicken. Rosa threw rocks, sticks and whatever she could find after that devil, the coyote.

Poor old Tiger was still yelping in pain and trying to get up. It was impossible for him to finish chasing the coyote into the woods as they had planned. However, Coyote still was able to have a plump chicken to eat for his lunch. Rosa felt so sorry for Tiger and she felt so guilty, that she put her arms around him, holding him in sorrow and compassion.

Tiger tried to stand but kept falling over, whimpering in pain from where she had hit him with the gun. He wanted to say, "Take me back." Maybe Rosa understood him because she picked him up, carried him into the house and put him on the couch. Her touch felt like an angel to the old dog. Having her arms around him brought back wonderful memories of his puppy years when he had been allowed to sleep there occasionally.

"Come on, my hero..."

First, Mrs. Terrell called Dr. Miller, the veterinarian, who said, "Bring Tiger in as quickly as you can get here.

Next, Rosa wanted to tell Don the news, too. So, when she talked to him on the telephone, he was surprised to hear her story because he, too, had thought the problem with Tiger had been taken care of several days ago. When she told him about the gun not firing, he explained that he had forgotten to tell her that he had taken the bullets out of the rifle the day the grandchildren had visited. "Well, let me know what the vet says," Don said.

Then Rosa picked up the skinny old dog in her arms and said, "Come on, my hero, we're going to the vet. He'll make you all well again." Tiger had stopped crying and his biggest problem was that he was hungry more than anything else—although his leg did hurt quite a bit.

Back in the woods, Coyote stood watching the house. He saw the mistress carrying Tiger to the house and later to the car. Smiling to himself, he decided that the plan had worked well so far even if Tiger had been unable to chase him. He was happy to see them drive away in the car because he was planning to have another chicken for dinner — maybe two.

When they arrived at the veterinarian's clinic, Rosa described the fight to the doctor. "I have never seen such a fight," she said. "They must have been rolling around, snapping and growling at each other for thirty minutes. Tiger was so tired and injured that he couldn't even stand up," she said patting her hero dog on the head very softly and talking in a very gentle voice. The old dog continued to whimper and whine a little, but whether it was from pain or happiness, no one could tell.

The doctor checked Tiger all over and said, "He doesn't seem to have any broken bones, and I don't see any bites either. That seems a bit unusual for such a hard fight and especially for such a long time. I can't find a single scratch. He only has a bad bruise on his leg from where you hit him with the rifle." He stroked Tiger in a friendly and reassuring way.

"That is odd, isn't it?" remarked Tiger's mistress. "However, I was a witness to the whole thing myself and I saw that coyote run off into the woods after Tiger got through with him. Well, I want him looked at very carefully in case that coyote had rabies or something," said Rosa. "Maybe he should stay here overnight just in case we miss something that shows up later. He's due for his shots anyway and a good bath, too. Let's give him the full treatment. He's my hero dog today.

"May I ask a favor, please? May I use your telephone to call my husband? He'll want to know how Tiger is when you're finished."

"Of course, Mrs. Terrell."

Don was glad to hear that Tiger had only a bruise, but he still couldn't understand about the old dog. He had paid fifty dollars to have him shot a few days ago. How had Tiger found his way home? And what had happened to the men that Don had paid to do the job? He wanted to find out the answers to his questions as soon as possible.

Rosa wanted to reward her hero, so, before she went home, she went to the store to buy some ground beef. Taking it back to the clinic, she asked Dr. Miller to give it to Tiger because he had earned it. The doctor could tell that the poor dog had not had very much nutritious food for a long time, so he was glad that Rosa had brought some good meat for him. Tiger gobbled it up realizing how different life can be from one day to the next. But in his heart, he was thanking his friend, Coyote.

That evening at home, Mr. Terrell was still trying to figure out what had happened. He wasn't sure if his wife had done something to trick him into keeping the old family pet. "I told you we were going to get rid of him and I paid those guys fifty dollars to do it. So why is he still here, Rosa?"

"I'm not sure how he managed to come back home, and I don't care how much you paid to have him shot. He's back home and this is where he is going to stay. He tried to defend our home, he fought with a coyote and he protected our chickens today and that's all there is to it," argued Rosa.

Don went to the telephone. Something had obviously gone wrong with his deal with Bob who was one of the raccoon hunters. "Hello, is this Mr. Guzman? This is Don Terrell," he said after the person had answered, "I'm sorry to bother you, but do you know where I can find another good dog?"

"Well, no. We only have 'coon hunters. If we run across one, though, we can give you a call. Okay?" said the voice on the other end.

"Thanks," said Don, "and, by the way, did you have any problems getting rid of Tiger, my old dog? Did he give you any trouble?"

"A..a..no...not really. We picked him up at your house and took him very deep into the woods and shot him just like you wanted. And that's not all," the man continued, " we dug a hole and buried him, too."

"Well, you guys went through quite a lot. Do I owe you any more money since you even went to the trouble of burying him for me?" asked Don.

"That isn't necessary," came the reply, " but we can always use an extra ten if you're feeling generous," he said laughing a little.

By this time in their conversation, Don Terrell, who was accustomed to having things done his way, was more than a little irritated because he knew Mr. Guzman was lying to him. Without raising his voice, he asked, "I'm sorry, but I've forgotten your first name. What was it?"

"Bob. Bob Guzman, sir" he answered.

"Well, Bob Guzman, I don't much like someone who lies to me and I believe that's what you have been doing. My old dog is recovering from a fight with a coyote and is at the vet's right now." There was a long silence on the other end of the telephone.

"Well, I can tell you what happened, sir. I gave the job to somebody else and he told me he had done it."

"That's too bad for you, Bob, because a deal is a deal and you owe me fifty dollars and I want it in cash and the sooner the better. Bring it to me tomorrow after work." He added, " Thanks for nothing."

"Please, sir, let me come and get the dog and I guarantee…"

"Forget it, Bob. Just bring me my money." Mr. Terrell hung up.

Later, Rosa was concerned about the coyotes coming again and suggested that a fence be put all around the property. However, Don knew that it would be far too expensive to fence four acres of land. "Besides," her husband reminded her, "the new German shepherd will be here in a couple of days and our coyote troubles will be over for sure."

Chapter Thirteen

The next day, when Don Terrell returned home from work, Tiger had returned home, too, from the vet's. Life was much different now than it had been just a few days earlier. He'd had a bath, had eaten some good meals and had his rabies shots and even the fleas were all gone. He felt like a new dog and truly enjoyed his new situation.

It was two days later when the new dog arrived. Mr. Terrell was right; he was a big dog and made himself at home by marking his territory in just the same way that Tiger had always done. At first, Tiger was a little jealous, but the German shepherd was so young and had such a great disposition that soon, they were getting along well enough to eat out of the same dish. They both had the same mission: protect the home and all the property.

Tiger, however, was concerned about his part of the plan regarding the chickens and the coyote. He wanted to uphold the bargain, but with the new dog around, it would not be easy. He wished he could talk with his friend, Coyote, to warn him but since he couldn't do that, Tiger made a deal with the young dog that might help Coyote, too.

"I'll work days and you can work nights," he told the big pup. The young shepherd agreed. But this was not a great plan for the coyote because he didn't know about the new dog. However, the coyote was cleverer than the young dog and would certainly be able to catch a chicken or two before the German shepherd became more experienced.

That night, the shepherd dog was on duty for the first time, just as the coyote came quietly walking through the foggy night air. Coyotes have good eyes, but with so much fog, he was not expecting to find such a large new dog looming up ahead of him. The shepherd was excited by the challenge of facing a coyote and having to chase him away from his territory. So, when the dog encountered the surprised coyote, he didn't ask questions. Their fight was over in minutes because the coyote, although clever, recognized the large size of the new guardian and escaped, quickly slipping off into the fog and disappearing among the shadows of the trees.

The German shepherd called out to Tiger who was sleeping in his usual resting place under the porch, "Hey, Tiger, come here. Help me catch that intruder. It's a coyote, but he's getting away. Can you help me?" he asked.

But Tiger only yawned, turned around, tucked his nose under his tail to keep warm and went back to sleep. After all, he wasn't on duty. He was retired. This was how he could keep his agreement—how he could complete the plan with his good friend, Coyote. He would never have to chase the coyotes again. And the old dog didn't really want to help catch his friend. In fact, he never will.

- The End -

Some True Facts about the Coyote

The coyote is a wild, dog-like animal that lives in almost every part of the United States. They are especially abundant in the southwestern states: Oklahoma, Colorado, New Mexico, Arizona, California, Texas and in northern Mexico. They manage to live in the mountains as well as the plains. Almost any environment allows the coyote to survive because they are so clever or cunning. Because man has tried so many ways to get rid of them, the coyote has become very wary and has learned to elude or avoid almost every method man has tried.

For food, they hunt for prairie dogs, rabbits, rats, mice—even snakes—to survive. Chickens and ducks are not safe from this sly hunter, either. Occasionally, they will bring down a sheep, goat or a young calf and have even been known to attack a small pony when they are more desperate for food. When they are near peoples' homes, they will try to eat any food or garbage left unattended. People are cautioned not to leave pet food outside and to keep all garbage well contained. A coyote will scavenge for dead animals—carrion—and will eat berries and fruit. They are often clever enough to even eat melons.

You may wonder why eating melon is considered a clever thing to do. In some places where farmers grow watermelon, the coyote will be the first to eat the ripe melon because they *never* take a bite of a green melon. Somehow, they know exactly which ones are already ripe and which ones are still green before they feast on the succulent fruit.

The coyote is one of the most clever and wily of all animals that manages to survive in the wild.

Review Questions

1. Can you explain the difference between a wild animal and a domestic animal?

2. Why did Mr. Terrell want to get rid of his dog, Tiger?

3. What animal will not allow itself to be blinded by a flashlight when it's dark out?

4. Can you remember how the coyote gets the chickens down from the trees?

5. What prevented Mrs. Terrell from shooting the coyote?

6. How does the coyote trick the shepherd when it is trying to get his goats?

7. How much did Mr. Terrell pay to get rid of his dog?

8. How does the coyote manage to get rid of his fleas?

9. How did Mr. Terrell break his arm?

10. What was the veterinarian's last name?

(Review questions continued)

11. What kept the coyote from killing the old dog when he first saw him?

12. What kind of fight was planned between the old dog and the coyote?

13. What was the name of the raccoon hunter?

14. What did the old dog realize when the coyote was instructing him?

15. Who is the coyote's worst enemy?

16. What was the wise advice the coyote gave to the old dog?

17. What were the first names of Mr. and Mrs. Terrell?

18. What type or breed of dog was going to replace Tiger?

19. Why the coyote must be so clever?

20. Where did the old dog hide and sleep when he was still at home?

The Author

Adán Zepeda was born in Ricardo, Texas, in 1935. He was raised in Mexico until the age of fifteen and attended school—at the age of ten—for only one year and a half. He didn't return to school the next year because he had to work in the fields to help support the family. When his father passed away. Adán and his family moved back to the United States near the South Texas border where he became a farm worker.

Without knowing a word of English, he was afraid to meet anyone who could not also speak his language, Spanish. In the 1960's, his cousin taught him the alphabet but nothing more.

When he traveled to the West Side of Texas, he went with his Uncle Silvano. The two of them were looking for better cotton fields to earn a little more money. Of course, this was only a temporary season—with no future.

In 1973, Adán and his wife moved to Northern Indiana, still looking for a better tomorrow for their son and daughters. Five years later, he was invited to attend a weekend retreat in Chicago. During the event, all the people were encouraged to write a paragraph using a topic from one of the sessions. Following that weekend, he was inspired to write on a regular basis, first poems and then short stories. More than 200 poems are included in his first book, *Lagrimas y sonrisas.* Other books in both Spanish and English now include *Apples for Life, Manzanas por Vida, The Mouse Ark* and the latest one, *The Old Dog and the Coyote.*

The Illustrator

Nancy Glon was born in Indianapolis, Indiana, in 1936. Her drawing skills were begun at an early age, but were only developed later in life. While raising a large family, often working outside the home and being involved in church and community efforts, it was sometimes difficult to continue her several hobbies. They included calligraphy, (wedding invitations and personalizing), portraiture, "Gold Bricks" and, of course, illustrating children's books.

When she and her husband moved to Goshen, Nancy met author, Adán Zepeda and a cooperative friendship developed. Over a period of about two years, she illustrated his book, *Apples for Life,* and revised some of her drawings for the Spanish edition, *Manzanas por vida.* She has illustrated *The Mouse Ark* for Mr. Zepeda, the first of a series of four books. The two continue to work on other stories written by him which include this book about the coyote and an old dog.